# Search and Rescue

## Penn Mullin

A **PERSPECTIVES** BOOK
**High Noon Books**
**Novato, California**

Series Editor: Penn Mullin
Cover and Illustrations: Herb Heidinger

International Standard Book Number: 0-87879-292-9

9  8  7  6  5  4  3  2
20 19 18 17 16 15 14 13

You'll enjoy all the High Noon Books. Write for
a free complete list of titles.

# Contents

# Chapter 1

# The Search is On!

"There's a search! Six-year-old boy. He's been missing since morning on Mount Asher. Bad storm on the way. Get here as soon as you can. We'll meet at the main parking lot on Mount Asher at six."

"Right, Dave," Rick said. Then he hung up the phone. Here it was at last—his first search! He'd been waiting a long time for this. Ever since last winter when he joined the Search and Rescue group. Now it wasn't practice any more—this was for real.

Rick pulled on a sweater. There was no way to tell when he would get home again. It was a big mountain.

He went into the garage to get his pack. It hung on the wall, all set to go. Better double check it, Rick thought.

Sleeping bag
Pack tent
Mess kit and packs of dried food
Water bottle
Matches
Rope
Extra clothes
Compass
Flashlight and extra batteries
Knife
First aid kit
Emergency kit

All the things he'd need. Rick hurried outside with the pack. There was no time to lose. He had less than an hour till he had to meet his Search and Rescue group on the mountain.

His dark blue VW sat in the driveway. Rick threw his pack into the trunk. His boots, jacket, and helmet were already there. He started the engine. Full tank. Good thing he'd gassed up on the way home from work. He could see Mount Asher far ahead. It was high, dark, and green. Huge, thought Rick. It must be covered with a million trees! And one little boy up there—somewhere—all alone.

Rick thought about all the times he had gone camping with his mother and father and his sister

A million trees! And one little boy up there—all alone.

Laura. They had always had such great times! They had spent many nights on the side of a mountain. And those trout streams. I was only five or six when we first went camping, thought Rick. I would have been scared to death if I had been lost. That poor little kid.

Rick looked at his watch. Not many hours of daylight left. He could see dark storm clouds at the top of the mountain. Suddenly he felt it coming—the old feeling. He shivered. No, he couldn't let it stop him. Not now. He'd trained so hard to be ready for a search. The group was waiting for him. They *must* not find out his secret. Rick pushed down hard on the gas pedal. He was getting closer to the mountain. And the sky got darker.

# Chapter 2

# The Challenge

Rick drove into the parking lot on Mount Asher. The sky was very dark. The storm was only minutes away. Suddenly he heard thunder. For a moment he felt like turning around. He could go back down the mountain. Away from the storm. Then he saw his friends Dave and Sara waving at him. They were unloading their cars. Rick waved and pulled in next to Dave's van.

"Hey, Rick, glad you could make it," Sara said.

"Welcome aboard! What a night for your first search!" Dave said. "Better hurry and get your gear unpacked. We'll be heading out soon."

"Right," Rick said. He looked up at the sky. He felt a light mist on his face. Thunder rumbled again. He started unloading the VW. If only the storm would move away from the mountain!

"Attention, everybody! Gather round." A tall

A tall man in a dark green jacket was talking through a bullhorn.

man in a dark green jacket was talking through a bullhorn. He stood in the middle of the parking lot. This was Matt Johnson, the Field Leader. Other members of Search and Rescue were standing around him. Rick, Dave, and Sara went to join them.

"Thanks for coming out tonight," Matt said.

"I know it's going to be rough. Night search in a storm. But you're ready. You've shown it in training. I know we can count on you. The sheriff's men searched all day for the boy. No luck. So they called us. Too bad they waited till almost dark. With an earlier start we'd have him by now.

"The boy's name is Timmy Scott. Black hair, blue eyes. And he's pretty big for six. First reported missing at nine this morning. Walked away from his parents' camp right over there." Matt pointed to a group of tall pines.

"Timmy has no food on him. No jacket either. Just jeans and a t-shirt. This means trouble. It's been getting colder all afternoon. Let's hope this storm passes over. If it doesn't, things look bad for Timmy. Hypothermia could kill him fast."

Hypothermia. Rick shivered as he heard the word. He'd learned about hypothermia in basic search training. It is called the silent killer. The body gets colder and colder — then, death. Hypothermia could kill even on a summer afternoon. If a person gets wet and then chilled in a cold wind, hands and feet get numb. Then the cold spreads to the inside of the body. Blood begins to flow away from the brain itself. The person becomes confused and soon cannot walk or stand. Hypothermic people usually never know what is happening to them. And when their brains stop working, there is no way they can save themselves.

Cold, wind, and rain. Deadly when all together. They were here on this mountain. Timmy *had* to be found. Fast. The team was trained in first aid for hypothermia — how to get the body's temperature up as fast as possible. If only they could find Timmy in time . . .

"OK now. Get set to move out. Remember to keep close together in your line as you search." Matt's voice boomed out of the bullhorn. "Keep calling Timmy's name. And talk to each other. It's easy to get lost in that darkness. Timmy has been missing nine hours now. So every minute counts. Timmy is in great danger. He may die up there on the mountain."

# Chapter 3

# Lightning

Matt read the list of names for each search team. Rick listened for his name. Good. He was on Dave's team with Sara and Andy. He liked working with them. But Sid's name was also read. Sid had been trouble all through training. He was a great big guy with a wise mouth. Always bugging people about stupid things. Rick wished Sid wasn't on his team. Not tonight. Not in this storm.

"OK, everybody, get your packs on," Dave said. He'd been a team leader for three years. Rick had trained under him all spring. Dave was fair to everybody. He was older but he wasn't stuck on himself. He'd taught Rick a lot about mountain rescue.

The team started putting on jackets, packs, and helmets. Sara was the team medic and wore a special first-aid pack.

Lightning flashed somewhere above them on the mountain. Rick felt tight all over. He waited for the crash of thunder. There it was, getting closer now.

"We'll start right here and move up the creek," Dave said. "Timmy might have followed it. His mother said he loves to play in water. That could be bad. He can't swim." Rick felt a chill go down his back. The thought of Timmy's body in the creek was terrible. He *had* to be found—alive! Rick was ready to get going on the search.

"Stay fifteen feet apart. Keep your eyes and ears open. Look *all* around you. Up and behind. Call Timmy's name. Let's go!"

Dave spread the team out in a line: Sid, Rick, Sara, and Andy. He followed along a few yards behind them. The other search teams moved out, too. They went in other directions on the mountain.

The woods were already dark. The only sound was the wind in the trees. And the team's footsteps in the leaves. Thunder rumbled somewhere high on the mountain. Rick tried to keep his mind on only the trail ahead. He used his flashlight in a wide circle as he walked. Any minute now, would his light find a small body on the ground?

"Timmy! Timmy!" the searchers kept calling. Their voices couldn't be heard far. It was getting too windy.

"Hey, Rick, how's it going?" Andy called out.

"OK. Just hope the storm holds off," Rick shouted back.

"You calling me, Rick?" Sid yelled. He was about ten feet to Rick's left. "Don't be scared. I won't leave you!" He laughed.

"Cool it, Sid," Rick tried to yell above the wind.

Suddenly the woods were filled with bright light. Thunder crashed down around the team. Rick couldn't move. He wanted to run. But where? Lightning flashed again. Rick could see Sid moving on ahead. The thunder boomed. Rick still couldn't move. Suddenly it all seemed like that terrible night of the accident last year. He would never forget the way the lightning had flashed all around the car. He would never forget feeling the car slip over the edge of the road. And how scared his sister was when the car started to slide.

Rick still stood there on the mountain trail. Rain had begun to fall. It beat down hard on his helmet.

"Come on, Rick!" Sid yelled. "You're holding

He wanted to run. But where? Lightning flashed again.

up the line. You chicken or something?"

Another huge crack of lightning. It's right on top of me, Rick thought. Any minute I'll be hit and that will be the end! Just the way that tree was the night of the wreck. He'd never forget seeing a giant bolt of lightning tear a tree in two. Right in front of the car as it lay on its side in the mud. He'd known he had to get out of that car.

Go get help for Laura. She had hit her head and had passed out. But he hadn't gone for help. He had just sat there while lightning flashed around the car. He and Laura were found hours later. "Why didn't you go for help?" the police had asked Rick. "Your sister's in bad shape."

"Rick, come on! What's wrong with you?" He heard Sid shouting and remembered where he was. On the search on Mount Asher. "Hey, everybody, Rick's scared of a little lightning!" Sid yelled down the trail.

Rick just stood there. He couldn't stop shaking. He *was* scared, but he didn't want anyone to know it.

# Chapter 4

# The Truth

Suddenly Rick felt an arm go around his shoulder.

"Hey, it's OK, Rick. Take it easy. Lightning's no fun." Dave had come up behind Rick. Sid, Sara, and Andy were standing on the trail ahead. "Your mouth is too big for your head, Sid!" Dave shouted. "Let's rest, everybody."

Dave led the team to a dry spot under a high shelf of rocks. He pulled out a candy bar and offered it to Rick.

"No thanks. I don't know what—" Rick began.

"No problem. OK now?" Dave asked.

"Think so. Sorry about back there."

"Ever have any problems with lightning before, Rick?" Dave asked.

Rick looked at his teammates. He knew they were listening. This was going to be tough.

"Yes. Last year. There was a wreck."

Dave led the team to a dry spot under a high shelf of rocks.

"Bad one? In a storm?" Dave asked.

"Yes. Our car slid off the road at night."

"Anybody hurt?"

"My sister. She hit her head. We didn't know if she would live."

"You were OK?"

"Yes, I was OK," Rick answered.

"Did they find you quickly?" Sara asked.

"No." Rick looked down at the ground.

"Want to talk about it?" Dave asked.

Rick's voice felt funny. It was hard to make the words come. "I didn't go for help."

There was a very long silence. Then Dave spoke. "You thought you better stay with your sister." Yes. Sure. That made sense. Why not say that was the reason? But suddenly Rick knew he wanted to be straight with Dave. And straight with his team.

"No. That wasn't it. It was the lightning." There. He'd said it. Now Dave will tell me I don't belong in Search and Rescue, Rick said to himself.

"So you stayed put. How about Laura?" Dave asked.

"She was in the hospital a long time," Rick said. He couldn't look at anyone.

"Guess you felt it was all your fault," Dave said.

"Yes. That's right," Rick told him.

"Well, it's time to quit blaming yourself," Dave said. "Get ahead of it. And remember — there's nothing wrong with being afraid. Everybody's got *something* they're scared of. With me it's — would you believe — spiders!"

Everybody laughed.

"No kidding?" Rick asked.

"Sure thing. Now let's get going up the trail. We've got a lot of mountain to cover. Keep close together as you walk. Keep calling Timmy's name. Remember — this storm could be deadly for him. Let's go!"

Dave led the way back out into the rain. Rick couldn't believe it — Dave still wanted him on the team. He was still part of the search. But what about his teammates? Would they ever dare to trust him now?

## Chapter 5

# A Cry in the Night

Rain beat down on the searchers. They kept right on going, moving in a line of four. Dave stayed behind them as they worked up the mountain. As team leader he carried a radio in his pack. He used it to check in with base camp and tell them where his team was.

Branches tore at Rick's face. He had to push his way through thick brush. It would have been far easier just to stick to the trail. But who could tell if Timmy had stuck to it? The air was filled with crackling lightning. Don't think about it. Just keep going, he told himself. Stay even with the line.

"Timmy! Timmy!" the team called again and again. Nothing but silence. And the deep roll of thunder high above them.

Suddenly a terrible scream cut the air. Rick's heart pounded. Could that scream be human?

"Big cat, everybody. Keep on moving. Let's make lots of noise," Dave called out.

Mountain lion. Rick shivered. It was awful to think of Timmy out there alone somewhere in the night. They *had* to find him before it was too late.

Everyone started yelling. Noise was important to scare away the mountain lion. And maybe Timmy would hear them. But could they hear Timmy? Dave soon gave the signal to cut the noise. Rick waited for the awful scream to come again. But there was nothing. Only the sound of the rain against the trees.

Suddenly Rick heard something. There it was. A cry? Where was it coming from? Rick shone his flashlight in a wide circle. Rocks, bushes, leaves, logs. There was the sound again. Behind him. He turned and shone the light across the ground. There. A mound of dark clothes— Timmy! It had to be! Please let him be OK, Rick said to himself. Please!

"It's Timmy! I've got him!" Rick yelled as he ran towards the small body on the ground. He threw himself down beside the boy. Timmy lay on his back in the wet leaves. His eyes were closed. Rick put his ear to Timmy's chest. The heartbeat was there. But it wasn't strong.

There. A mound of dark clothes—Timmy! It had to be!

Timmy's clothes were sopping wet. His skin felt
icy cold. Rick felt for Timmy's pulse. Slow. Very
slow. Suddenly there was a huge flash of lightning. Rick didn't even notice. In the light from
the flash he could see the blue color of Timmy's
skin. Hypothermia. The quiet killer. All the signs
were there.

# Chapter 6

# A Life to Save

The rest of the team rushed to Rick's side.

"Great going, Rick," Dave said as he knelt beside Timmy. "How is he?"

"It looks bad," Rick answered. "Weak pulse, icy cold, blue skin. Hypothermia. I'm sure of it."

"How did he even make a noise?" Andy asked.

"You've got great ears, Rick," Sara said. "If you hadn't heard him . . ."

"Got to get those wet clothes off him," Dave said.

Rick started taking off Timmy's soggy T-shirt. He would never forget how cold and clammy the boy's skin felt. Andy pulled dry clothes for Timmy from his own pack. Sara and Sid helped dress Timmy. Andy's clothes were huge on the small body, but it didn't matter. They would help him get warm. The wool hat was most important of all. Most of a person's body heat is lost through the top of his head.

Rick opened his pack tent. The others helped him put it up. They laid a sheet of plastic on the floor of the tent. They gently laid Timmy down on it. Then Rick unrolled his sleeping bag and got inside it. He needed to warm it up before Timmy was put in with him.

"I'll start my stove and make hot soup," Sid said. He found a safe place out of the rain under some thick trees.

Dave got on his radio to the base camp. "Team Four here. Found Timmy alive. Hypothermic. Very weak. Too risky to carry him down. Better send the chopper. We're five miles up from base camp. Just off Main North Trail. We'll check back with you soon as we find a good landing place. Over."

Andy and Sara lifted Timmy into the sleeping bag beside Rick. Rick put his arms around him and hugged him hard. He had seen this done in drills so many times. This was for real now. Timmy's life was on the line. The small body felt icy cold. Rick hoped his own body heat would soon warm up Timmy. It *had* to. If Timmy's temperature got as low as 78°, he would die. Rick looked at Timmy's face. Still no color. Still unconscious. Breathing slow.

"I'll get in there on the other side of Timmy," Sid said. He squeezed himself into the bag. Now Timmy was getting heat from both sides.

"Is he getting any warmer?" Sara asked. She knelt inside the tent and felt Timmy's pulse.

"Not yet. I'll rub his back," Rick said. "You rub his hands, Sid."

"I'm sure getting hot in here!" Sid laughed. "Sure hope Timmy is."

"They're going to send up the chopper. We have to find a landing spot for it first," Dave said. "Andy, you go up ahead and look for a place big enough for the chopper to land in. Needs to be fifty to a hundred feet wide."

"Right. I'll take off now," Andy said. He picked up his flashlight and headed up the trail.

"This soup's nearly ready." Dave knelt over the tiny pack stove near the tent.

"We've got to get Timmy conscious first," Sara said. "Or he can't drink the soup. Any chance, Rick?"

"I *think* he feels warmer! How are his hands, Sid?"

"Better. I can feel a change. And—look at his eyes! I think he's waking up!" Sid cried.

Timmy lay on his back now between Sid and Rick. The boys bent over him, watching his face.

Map of the search area. Search began at the parking lot and rescue finshed at helicopter landing area.

"Come on, Timmy, wake up," said Sid. "Talk to us. You can do it, old buddy."

Rick rubbed Timmy's arms and legs to get the blood warmed and moving. I can't think of another thing to do, he thought. Why isn't he coming to?"

Suddenly Timmy's eyes moved, then opened wide. He blinked at Rick and Sid.

"Hooray, he's awake!" cried Rick.

# Chapter 7

# To the Clearing

Timmy's eyes stared at the two faces looking down at him.

"Don't be scared, Timmy," Rick said. "You're safe now. We found you. We'll get you back with your mom and dad soon as we can."

Timmy's teeth began to chatter. His body started shaking.

"Hold on tight. We're trying to warm you up," Rick told him. He put his arms around Timmy and hugged him close. Sid hugged him from the other side. They could feel Timmy's body slowly start to relax. The terrible cold was gone now. Timmy's temperature must be coming up. But he wasn't out of danger yet. No one knew how low his temperature had gone. He had to be moved to a hospital.

"Let's get this hot soup in him," Sara said. She bent down at the front of the tent. A steaming cup of soup was in her hand.

Rick and Sid pulled Timmy to help him sit up. Timmy just stared at the cup. He wouldn't open his mouth. And his eyes began to close again.

"C'mon, Timmy. Try this. Don't go to sleep on us," Sid said. He held the cup up to Timmy's mouth. But the boy's eyes stayed closed and he wouldn't open his mouth.

"Timmy, guess what! You're going to get to ride in a helicopter!" Rick told him. "You don't want to be asleep when the chopper comes."

Timmy opened his eyes and looked at Rick. Then he opened his mouth. Rick quickly gave him a sip of soup. Dave, Sara, and Sid cheered when they saw Timmy swallow. But after only a little bit he fell back into the sleeping bag.

"He's too weak to eat," Sara said. "This is what happens to people with hypothermia. They lose their will to live. We've got to get him down to the hospital. Fast."

Just then Andy came back down the trail. "There's a good clearing five hundred yards ahead," he said. "Right where the creek comes in. Should be fine for the chopper."

"Great. I'll radio base camp and let them know," Dave said. He used his flashlight to look at a map of the mountain. Then he took out his microphone. It was hooked by a wire to the radio in his pack. "Team Four here. Timmy is awake now. Needs emergency treatment. Bring chopper in where Big Fork Creek cuts across Main North Trail. There's a good clearing there. Watch for our fires. We're on our way there now. Over."

Rick and Sid got out of the sleeping bag. Then they zipped Timmy up tight inside it. They covered him with a sheet of plastic. Then they took down the tent and put it back in Rick's pack. Sara used her jacket to keep the rain off Timmy's face. She felt his pulse. Weaker. Things didn't look good.

"Let's get moving," Dave said.

"I'll take Timmy." Rick bent down to pick up the boy. "C'mon, big guy. Ready to see that chopper?" Rick picked up the sleeping bag with Timmy inside it.

"You've got your hands full. I'll carry your flashlight for you," Sid said.

They all set off up the trail following Dave. Sid shone the flashlight on the ground ahead of Rick. The rain didn't stop. Timmy's face was very wet now. Rick could hear his teeth beginning to chatter again. This was bad. Timmy *must* not lose all the heat they had worked so hard for. Rick looked down at the boy. His eyes were open again. He stared up at Rick.

"Almost there, Timmy. Help me listen for that chopper. It's coming to get you," Rick said. "Don't go to sleep."

Rick's arms began to hurt as the trail got steeper. But he had to keep climbing up that hill.

"Want me to take him for awhile?" Andy called back.

"No. We're fine," Rick answered. "Thanks."

He hoped the clearing was close now. The rain had chilled him, too. He shivered as his ears strained for the sound of the helicopter.

Suddenly there was a blinding flash of lightning. The woods were lit up bright as day. Thunder boomed. The whole mountain seemed to shake. Timmy cried out. His arms reached out of the sleeping bag and grabbed onto Rick's neck.

"It's OK. I've got you," Rick said. "Makes a lot of noise, doesn't it? Want to help me listen for the helicopter?"

He looked down at the boy. Timmy's face was right next to Rick's jacket. His arms still held onto Rick's neck. Rick's back hurt. He could hand Timmy over to Sid for awhile. But he knew Timmy didn't want to let go. Lightning crackled again. He felt Timmy's body get tight. He could tell that Timmy was scared, too. And he knew that he would somehow keep carrying the boy all the way to the clearing.

"I don't like the looks of this," Dave yelled to the team. "The storm's right above us. Might keep the chopper from landing."

It was a horrible thought. What if they had to *carry* Timmy back down the mountain tonight? That would mean hours until he could reach the hospital. The chopper *had* to be able to land. Rick kept listening for the sound of the engines.

"Almost there," Andy shouted above the wind. Rick could see an opening in the trees ahead. The clearing.

Suddenly they all heard it. There was no mistake. The steady chop-chop-chop sound of the chopper's motor. It got closer and closer.

"There it is, Timmy! The helicopter's almost here." Rick forgot about how heavy Timmy was. All he wanted to do now was to get to that clearing.

Dave reached the clearing first. He lit flares to signal the chopper. The whirring sound of the rotors was coming closer and closer. Suddenly the team could see the lights of the helicopter. It came in low over the trees. Then it was right above them. Lightning lit up the sky and the

"There it is, Timmy! The chopper's almost here."

whole clearing. Rain came down hard. Would the chopper try to land? Once it touched the ground it would be a perfect target for the lightning. It was up to the pilot to decide.

# Chapter 8

# Deadly Target

The chopper was landing. The pilot would take a chance with the lightning. The team cheered as they watched the helicopter slowly lower itself. It set down in the clearing about a hundred feet away. The wind from the rotors tore at Rick's clothes.

Rick looked down at Timmy. The boy's eyes were wide open now. He stared at the chopper. "There it is, Timmy! It's going to take you down the mountain," Rick said.

"Now?" Timmy said it so softly Rick almost didn't hear it.

"You bet! Any minute!" Rick shouted above the sound of the engines. "Hey, Sara, everybody, Timmy just talked to me!"

Dave started to run out towards the front of the chopper. He was careful to keep his head low. The team could see him talking to the pilot. Then he came running back. Lightning flashed all around him. It was a long way across the clearing. Thunder boomed.

"Rick," Dave shouted, "you go with Timmy in the chopper. You're the one who found him. The rest of us will walk down. Not enough room. Better go *now*. Chopper has to get off the ground. Lightning's bad."

"OK, Timmy. Ready to run?" Rick kept his arms around the boy.

The chopper looked miles away. An open hundred feet where lightning flashed again and again.

Dave touched Rick's shoulder. "Great job, Rick. Glad you're on my team."

"Take it easy, Rick," Andy said.

Sara hugged Timmy and Rick. "You're both terrific!"

"See you down there. Take care, OK?" Sid straightened Rick's helmet for him.

It was time to go. Rick and Timmy started out across the clearing. It was hard to move fast. Timmy's body in the sleeping bag was a big load. The rain beat against their faces. The wind tore at their bodies. And lightning crackled all around them. Rick could feel Timmy's nails digging into the skin of his neck. They kept on going towards the chopper. It seemed to take forever. Every

Lightning crackled. Rick could feel Timmy's nails digging into the skin of his neck.

second the chopper sat on the ground was bad. It could be hit by lightning. Rick and Timmy were perfect targets, too, as they moved across the open clearing.

Almost to the chopper now. The wind from the rotors blasted them. They bent their heads down low as they went under the whirling blades.

They reached the open door. A pair of arms reached down for Timmy. But the boy wouldn't let go of Rick. Someone finally had to pull them on board together. Then the chopper rose and headed down the mountain. Away from the storm.

# Chapter 9

# Race Against Time

Rick sat beside the chopper pilot. He looked out the window. There was nothing but darkness outside. When would they reach the hospital? Rick turned around to look at Timmy. He was lying on a stretcher on the floor of the helicopter. Bob, the medic, sat beside him. Timmy's eyes were closed. He had passed out again. Rick became very worried.

"We're almost there," said Al, the pilot. "We'll be at the hospital any minute. They'll be ready for us."

"Every minute counts," said Bob. "Good thing you found Timmy when you did, Rick. Another hour or two out in that storm and he'd have been a goner. Even now we can't be sure he'll pull through."

He's *got* to live, Rick said to himself. He's made it this far. Come on, Timmy. Hang in there. Just a little bit longer now.

Rick looked down at Timmy. Bob had taken the boy out of the sleeping bag and wrapped him tightly in blankets. The blue wool hat was still on his head. His face was white, too white. How much more time did they have?

Rick felt the chopper suddenly dip lower. Now he could see lights from the window. How wonderful they looked!

"We can set down right by the hospital's emergency door," Al said. "Rick, help me look for their lights. We're almost over the hospital. They'll be flashing red lights."

Rick could see the hospital now. All its windows were lit up. What a sight it was! And there were the flashing red lights, too.

"Right down there, Al. There's the light we must use to land," Rick said.

"Here we go." Al slowly brought the helicopter down. He drew closer to the flashing red lights. Then he gently touched down on the ground. The giant blades slowed to a stop. Everything was quiet. People in white uniforms rushed towards the chopper. The door was open, and Timmy was gently unloaded on his stretcher. He was still unconscious.

Rick jumped down and followed Timmy into

Rick could see the hospital now. What a sight it was!

the hospital. The lights in the hallway glared brightly in Rick's eyes. He kept following Timmy's stretcher. It had been placed on a cart with wheels now. It was pushed quickly through the hallway. Everyone seemed to know there was no time to lose.

In the emergency room doctors and nurses were all around Timmy. Rick and Bob stood outside in the hallway.

"We'll let you know how he's doing as soon as we know something," Bob said. "Why don't you go get a Coke? Take it easy for awhile. The doctors are going to raise Timmy's temperature. That's the most important thing to do right now."

"How will they do that?" Rick asked.

"I think they're going to try giving him warm oxygen. This gets him warm from the inside out," Bob said. Then he left Rick and went into the emergency room.

Rick wished he could go with Bob. It was awful not knowing how Timmy was doing. It seemed wrong that he had to wait out here. After all, hadn't he been the one who found Timmy? If only the rest of the team were here right now, Rick thought. But that was impossible. They were still on their way down the mountain. Rick sat down to wait in the hallway. He felt very alone and very scared.

# Chapter 10

# Night's End

Someone was shaking Rick's shoulder. "Wake up! I've got good news!" It was Bob's voice. Rick sat up straight in his chair. He was wide awake now.

"Timmy! He's OK?"

"Going to be fine. He's awake now. Temperature's up. Look's good," Bob said.

"Fantastic!" Rick cried. "When can I see him?"

"In just a few minutes. First, there's some people here who want to meet you." Bob stepped aside.

"We're Timmy's parents," said a pretty brown-eyed woman. Rick hadn't noticed her standing behind Bob.

"We've got a lot to thank you for, Rick," said Timmy's father. He was a tall, strong man. Timmy looked like him. "If you hadn't found Timmy when you did . . ." He put out his hand to Rick.

Some one was shaking Rick's shoulder. "Wake up! I've got good news."

Rick stood up and took Mr. Scott's hand. "I'm glad to meet you, sir. Timmy's a great little guy. Must have had you really scared when he disappeared."

"It was horrible," said Timmy's mother. She covered her face with her hands. She was still in her camping clothes. They were torn and dirty now from searching for Timmy.

"When night came, we'd almost given up hope," Mr. Scott said. "Then your team showed up and took over. They sure are a terrific bunch, that Search and Rescue group."

"We just got to the hospital a little while ago," said Mrs. Scott. It took us a long time to get down the mountain road in the dark. Timmy woke up at dawn just before we got here."

"Want to come see him now, Rick?" Bob asked.

"You bet!" Rick followed Bob and Timmy's parents down the hallway.

Bob opened the door to a bright, sunny room. Timmy lay over by the window. He looked awfully small in the long white bed. His face lit with smiles when he saw his parents and Rick.

"Hey, Timmy! You look great," Rick said. "Give me five." Timmy put out his small hand. Rick covered it with his own.

"Where's the helicopter?" Timmy asked. His voice still sounded very weak.

"Back at the rescue station now," Rick answered. "It sure got us down here fast."

"It was neat," Timmy said.

Rick smiled. He knew Timmy had been unconscious for almost the whole ride.

"We'll take you to see the helicopter," Mr. Scott said. "Just as soon as you're strong again."

The door to the room opened. In came Dave and the rest of the search team.

"Hi, everybody! We're back," Dave said. "We made super time coming down the mountain. Say, Timmy, you look terrific!"

Sara rushed over and gave Timmy a hug. Then she gave Rick one, too. "Great going, Rick. We missed you on the way down the mountain."

Rick felt good inside. Sara was a terrific girl. He hoped they could both stay on the same search team this year.

Sid put out his hand to Rick. "You're one brave guy," he said. "Crossing that open field full of lightning took guts. And with Timmy in your arms, too!"

"Thanks, Sid. You guys are a pretty great team to have. We all did it together. We all helped Timmy make it," Rick said.

"We owe all of you our thanks," said Timmy's father. "You're a terrific group of people."

"Rick did the most, though, Mr. Scott," Andy said. "He carried Timmy straight up the mountain in his arms."

"We owe you the most thanks of all, Rick," said Timmy's mother. "It's because of you that Timmy was found. And because of you that he made it to the hospital in time."

"Rick, are you a hero?" asked Timmy.

"Oh, I don't know about that," said Rick.

"He sure is a hero," Dave said. Then he winked at Rick, "In more ways than one. And I'll bet this hero's hungry! Come on, Rick, lead the way to breakfast!"